D1643562

A catalogue record for this book is available
from the British Library

Published by Ladybird Books Ltd
A subsidiary of the Penguin Group
A Pearson Company

PETER RABBIT AND FRIENDS™

TWO BAD MICE

Ladybird

${O}$nce upon a time there was a very beautiful dolls' house. It belonged to two dolls called Lucinda and Jane.

One morning, Lucinda and Jane
went out for a ride in their pram.

As soon as they were gone, two
mischievous mice called Tom Thumb
and Hunca Munca peeped out of
their hole.

"Let's go and see what we can find!"
said Hunca Munca.

The mice ran straight to the dolls' house and Hunca Munca knocked on the door. There was no reply.

"There's no one at home," she told Tom. "Let's have a look inside!"

When they stepped inside, the mice could hardly believe their eyes. Everything in the house was just the right size for them! They squeaked with joy.

"Oh, look, Tom!" cried Hunca Munca when she saw the dining room. "What a beautiful dinner!"

"Yes," said Tom, "it's all ready – and for us!"

Tom Thumb set to work at once to carve the ham. But it was so hard that the knife crumpled.

"It's not boiled enough!" cried Tom Thumb. "You try, Hunca Munca."

But Hunca Munca couldn't cut the ham either.

The rest of the food was no better. "It's no use," said Tom Thumb, angrily. "It's not for eating. Let's smash it all up!"

"Yes, let's!" agreed Hunca Munca.

They threw the food on the floor and smashed it to bits. But the fish wouldn't break.

"Let's burn it on
the fire!" said Tom.
They put the fish onto the crinkly
paper fire in the kitchen, but it would
not burn either.

The two mice were now *very* puzzled.

Tom squeezed up the chimney to see what could be the matter. "There's no soot up here," he called down to Hunca Munca.

He peeped out of the top of the chimney to look around, then jumped right out of the chimney and into the bedroom!

Meanwhile, Hunca Munca had
another disappointment. She found
some jars labelled JAM, FLOUR,
SAGO and COFFEE on a dresser.
But when she turned them over there
was nothing inside except some red
and blue beads.

Then those naughty mice became *very* annoyed. They set to work to do all the mischief they could in the little house.

Hunca Munca was pulling feathers out of the dolls' bolster when she had an idea. "Tom," she said, "this would be a nice bed for us. Let's take this bolster back to our house!"

"Come along, Tom!" said Hunca Munca, as the two little mice pulled the bolster down the stairs.

"I hope this will be worth all the work!" puffed Tom.

It took them a long time and much huffing and puffing, and pushing and pulling, but at last they managed to get the bolster into their own little home.

"Oh, that's *lovely*!" exclaimed Hunca Munca, admiring their new feather bed. The children jumped up and down with excitement.

The mice scurried back to the dolls'
house to see if they could find
anything else that would be useful.

Hunca Munca fetched a little wicker
cradle. "This will be fine for my
babies!" she said, happily. They also
found a chair and a dustpan and
broom.

The mice were just taking a few more things from the house when the nursery door opened.

Lucinda and Jane had come back from their outing!

The mice hurried back to their hole,
taking as many things with them as
they could. They quickly tried to
push all their treasures inside.

What a sight met the eyes of Lucinda
and Jane when they returned home!
Everything was topsy-turvy and in a
terrible mess.

"Oh, no!" cried the little girl who owned the dolls' house. "What has happened here?"

"It must be mice," said the little girl's nurse, tutting.

"I shall get a doll dressed as a policeman!" said the little girl.

"And *I* will set a mousetrap!" decided the nurse.

Tom Thumb and Hunca Munca hadn't been able to squeeze everything they had brought from the dolls' house into their hole. But Hunca Munca had got the cradle for her babies and some of Lucinda's clothes. She had also collected some pots and pans and several other useful items.

Some time later, Tom Thumb showed
his children the trap the nurse had
set in the nursery. They had to be
very careful not to go near the
trap – or they could be in terrible
trouble!

Hunca Munca became quite good
friends with the policeman doll –
although he never said anything and
always looked quite stern.

In the end, the two bad mice were not so very naughty after all. Tom Thumb paid for everything he had broken. He found a crooked sixpence under the hearth rug...

And on Christmas Eve, he and
Hunca Munca stuffed it into one of
Lucinda and Jane's stockings.

And very early every morning, before
anybody is awake, Hunca Munca
comes with her dustpan and broom
to sweep the dolls' house!